STERLING CHILDREN'S BOOKS
New York

An Imprint of Sterling Publishing
1166 Avenue of the Americas
New York, NY 10036

STERLING CHILDREN'S BOOKS and the distinctive Sterling Children's Books logo
are trademarks of Sterling Publishing Co., Inc.

Text and illustrations © 2015 by Bryan Ballinger

ISBN 978-1-4549-1616-1

Distributed in Canada by Sterling Publishing
c/o Canadian Manda Group, 664 Annette Street, Toronto, Ontario, Canada M6S 2C8
Distributed in the United Kingdom by GMC Distribution Services
Castle Place, 166 High Street, Lewes, East Sussex, England BN7 1XU
Distributed in Australia by Capricorn Link (Australia) Pty. Ltd.
P.O. Box 704, Windsor, NSW 2756, Australia

For information about custom editions, special sales, and premium and corporate purchases,
please contact Sterling Special Sales at 800-805-5489 or specialsales@sterlingpublishing.com.

Manufactured in China
Lot #:
2 4 6 8 10 9 7 5 3 1
04/15

www.sterlingpublishing.com/kids

ANIMAL GAS

A FARTY FARCE

WRITTEN and ILLUSTRATED by Bryan Ballinger

STERLING CHILDREN'S BOOKS
New York

The End.